Dippers

WHITTEN HAGGARD, Des. et Del.

***Icticyon celiosylvestris*, dipper.**

(also water dog)

Note the ostentatious & erroneous absence of water

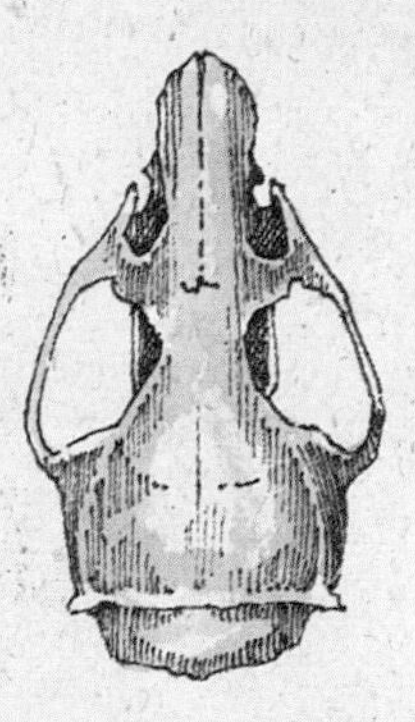

Skull of I. celiosylvestris, 1:2 1:1

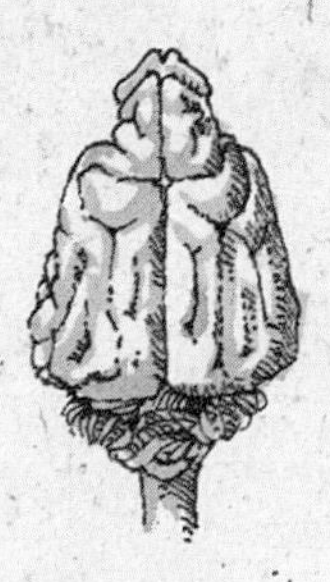

Brain of I. Celiosylvestris

Manus of I. celiosylvestris

Plate 926

Dippers

by Barbara Nichol

Illustrated by Barry Moser

TUNDRA BOOKS

For Claire Lawrence
B.N.

And for my friend Kate Kiesler
B.M.

Preface

THE WORDS in this book are reprinted from a letter, or rather a portion of a letter, housed in the archives of the City of Toronto.

The author of the letter is unknown, although, as we learn, her name was Margaret. In the summer of 1912—the summer she describes in the letter—she was about seven years old.

We don't know the identity of the person to whom the letter was sent. Neither do we know how the document made its way into the possession of the City of Toronto.

We do know that it entered the collection on April 19, 1973. That date is stamped on the envelope in which the letter is contained.

On that envelope is written by hand (and by whose hand, again, we do not know), "This is about the dippers that came up from the Don River."

Some sections of the original letter have been blacked out. This is the condition in which the document arrived at the archives.

The missing sections are marked by asterisks.

The spelling and punctuation have been corrected for the sake of clarity.

— BARBARA NICHOL

THERE was a little song the girls had for skipping. It went:

> Dipper dipper
> Come to stay
> Dipper dipper
> Fly away!

You'd jump into the skipping rope at the first part, and then when it went "Dipper dipper fly away," you'd jump out. Then it would be someone else's turn. Someone else would jump in.

We had that song even before the dippers came up from the river. Mother used to say to us, "Now, you girls don't go down to that river." The Don River was right there. Mother always thought something bad was going to happen. But you could go swimming down at the river and the boys could go fishing.

Louise and I could go there when we liked because Mother went to work. She cleaned house for people called the Cables up on Jarvis Street.

We lived on Mark Street, which was just off River Street. So we were right there. We were poor and that's where the dippers came around. They came up from the Don River.

Anyone who lived in that part of Toronto in those days knows about dippers. You don't see them now, but in those days they were nothing special. Aunt Benedict said they used to get them down in Windsor. She called them "water dogs." Across the river in Detroit they called them "paddies" or "water paddies."

It was when you got the hot weather that you got the dippers. We called it dipper weather. They'd come up out of the water down at the river. But the summer I'm talking about, they didn't just stay down at the river.

The summer the dippers came up was the same summer Louise got ill. That's how I remember it.

It was a very hot summer. There was a heat wave.

I was about seven or eight because I'd been to school already the year before. That made Louise five.

It was Louise and Mother and me. We didn't have any father. We lived in the back of the house. Upstairs, there were people called the O'Donnells.

* * *

The reason they were called dippers is because they'd fly back and forth just over the water and if you made a loud noise, they would dip down. If you clapped your hands, they'd dip down into the water.

They were frightened of the noise. We'd go down there and clap our hands to make them dip.

When you'd done it a few times, they'd dip down just a little in the air and come right back up. After a while they'd be on to you. They got used to the noise.

Sometimes the boys would throw rocks at them.

The dippers were maybe a foot long, or two feet. A big one would be bigger. They had the wings on their back. The wings were stubby and they weren't fur. They were like skin.

That's where the noise came from. It came from the wings. They made a noise when they were flying like clickety, clickety, clickety. They'd come out of the water and then they'd go back and forth, but not very high.

When they came up out of the water, the water would be running off them.

* * *

There was a story you heard before they came up that summer.

One lady came home from shopping and there was one that somehow got into her house. She didn't know it was there until it got stirred up and started bumping around inside. I think she scared it. This was before you knew to close the windows. She went running into the street. The boys were saying she went running into the street naked.

I don't know if that's true.

* * *

I remember Louise told me that the night she got sick she had a dream that she was flying. That's what she said later. Then when she woke up, she had the fever.

That was in the morning, and Mother thought it was just the heat bothering her so she went to work. It was my job to look out for Louise when Mother was at work.

But then later on in the morning, Louise was crying and rubbing her face and rubbing her eyes, and then she started bringing up. That was the beginning of it.

I could tell it wasn't from the heat. I told Mrs. O'Donnell from upstairs and she said, "Margaret, run up right away and get your mother at the Cables."

I can tell you for sure the dippers had come up by then because when I was going to get Mother they were saying on the street that there was a dipper hit by a streetcar in the night. It was a big one.

When we used to see them down at the river it looked like the fur was dark, but it turns out that's because they were wet. They looked dark and spikey. But now you could see that the fur was brown when it was dry. That dead one was the first one I saw close up.

That day when Louise got sick, Mrs. O'Donnell kept coming downstairs to talk to Mother, but she wouldn't come in the door. Mrs. O'Donnell worried about her Fiona catching something. Fiona O'Donnell had trouble with her breathing. Mrs. O'Donnell was always thinking she was going to catch something.

Mrs. O'Donnell was saying, "What's wrong with Louise? What's wrong with Louise?" but she wouldn't come in the door.

Then there was a nurse from the city who came by. Mrs. O'Donnell went up to the nurse and said, "Shouldn't the child be up in the Isolation Hospital?" Mother never forgave her for that. She held it against her.

When Louise got sick Mother had to stay home, so the Cables said she didn't have to come to work. They said, "We'll give you the money anyway. You take care of Louise."

But then Aunt Benedict came up from Windsor, and Mother went out part of the day to work someplace else. Mother kept up like that so she had the money from the two jobs. She didn't let on to the Cables. She didn't want to lose that job.

But she was always thinking the Cables would find out. She'd say, "If someone comes down here from the Cables, you just tell them I'm out downtown." When someone came near the house, I always thought it was someone from the Cables. I wished she just had the one job.

But you couldn't say that to Mother. Mother had a temper.

Aunt Benedict was an orphan. She was put on the steps of the orphanage. Then she was adopted.

This was something that happened to me.

I was going down the street and I kept hearing a rustling behind me. I kept looking around and looking around. I thought, "Well, I'm going crazy like everybody else."

Then I saw there was a dipper trying to keep up with me behind the hedge.

They had bright, shiny eyes. That's what you always hear, but it's true.

I don't remember where I was going.

* * *

There was something they used to have to keep the dippers from your house and that was dipper bells. You'd hang them near the front door to keep the dippers away, and then you'd hear them any time you had a breeze. People said dippers didn't like the tinkling noise.

Some people had them hanging all around their house and in the trees.

We had them because Aunt Benedict brought them up from Windsor.

But then some people said dippers liked the sound and would come to the bells instead of going away.

Maybe they worked and maybe they didn't. I don't know.

The dippers didn't want you going over to them. You'd see there would be people waiting for the streetcar and there would be a little crowd of dippers close by behind them.

But if anyone made out like they were going over to them, the dippers would just pick up off the ground to get away. You'd hear clickety, clickety. They didn't get up very high though. They'd go around something if they had the chance.

When you moved away, then they'd settle down. They didn't want you coming over.

There was a fellow who used to be up in Riverdale Park, where the zoo was. He'd be up there every day, and he would stand there and make a whistling noise. The dippers would go right over to him. They liked this noise he used to make. They'd come right up in front of his face. They called him Dipper Bill.

He was an old hobo. A big, heavy fellow.

Nobody would be looking at the animals at the zoo. Everyone would watch Dipper Bill, with the dippers all around his head. That was a strange thing. There would always be a crowd around him. He was a character. He was famous. You can find out about him.

The dippers had little legs hanging down, and when we saw them down on the river they looked like their legs didn't work. They looked like the legs were broken. When they came up, you saw they worked. That was a surprise. They could get along on them if they went slow.

Now I'll tell you something else from that summer. This is about Mother.

We were just walking on the street and she stopped to talk to a fellow. I don't remember anything special about the fellow, but afterwards she said to me, "That was your father back there."

I wish I had a better look. He looked too old to be our father. That was a strange thing, too.

Mother never talked about him at all. If she didn't want to talk about something, she wouldn't.

I used to say to her, "Maybe the Cables are going to see you coming home from work."

* * *

My idea was that Louise should be out back in a tent, like the fellows were when they had tuberculosis. They put those fellows out back of the houses in their own tents.

Mother said she wanted Louise where she could keep an eye on her. Louise had that leg that was going bad, and Mother had to get up in the night and rub it.

I had to sleep out on the porch by myself, because Mother didn't want me getting near Louise. And I couldn't have any light out there because the dippers would go for the light. Dippers didn't go away at night. Maybe there were more. I'd lie there quiet, but if I heard a dipper coming up close, I'd start in coughing. If they heard a noise, they'd go off the other way. I'd stay awake as long as I could because I didn't want them to bump against me.

Mother would come out and say, "You look like a raccoon with those dark circles."

If you went to sleep, you woke up because of the car horns. People had to go without their lights on. The dippers would go for the lights of the cars. They'd hit the dippers with the

cars. The people would turn off their lights and honk their horns to let people know they were there. Sometimes you'd hear the fellows let out a yell.

* * *

There was a dipper I saw down on River Street one time that had something wrong with it. It was in an empty lot and it couldn't fly off. It was going around and around on the little legs and it was dirty from the ground. There was a big crowd of children, because I wasn't the only one who saw him.

This one had a scratch on him. Maybe it got caught in some wire. Maybe it was a cat scratch. It'd go around and around and then it'd stop moving for a long time. Its eyes would close like it was squinting. You'd just see its chest huffing and puffing.

Then when it moved, all of us would run off. Then we'd come right back close.

It was there in the afternoon and then after supper. It was still there when it got dark, because all the children came back after supper. Then the next morning it was gone. Maybe somebody took it away.

I remember what people said. They said the dippers came from China. There'd been a boat from China in the harbor and the dippers came off the boat. That's where they came from at the first. That's what you'd hear. I guess they came from China. That's what I remember.

People would say things like, "Well, at least they don't bite" and "Well, at least they stay out of your way." You didn't know if they were going to stay for good. For all you knew, they were going to stay for good. People tried to make the best of it.

Then you'd hear, "Well, in five years' time there are going to be so many dippers they're going to be piled on top of each other and you won't be able to walk down the street."

So some people went one way in their thinking and some people went the other.

Then the dippers started to go away once the weather cooled off.

* * *

Louise used to make out that there was one time when one of them came in the house when we weren't paying attention.

She had a story that one day Aunt Benedict left the back door open by mistake and a dipper came in the house. She said it came right up to her on the bed, and she said she was petting it.

Louise said it came all the way in through the kitchen to the front room and then went all the way back out when we weren't paying attention. She said we didn't notice.

Mother said to me, "Just you let her say it. It doesn't hurt you." But they wouldn't come around you like that.

* * *

I had quite a scare one afternoon. This was after the dippers had mostly gone.

This young fellow came around the back of the house, and he was asking if Mother was home. He said, "Is Marjorie here?" He called Mother by her first name. Then he said he was Harry Cable. He was one of the Cable boys.

Louise was right there in the back, because she could sit out by then, and Mother was at her other job.

I remember when Harry Cable came by he was talking about Louise, too. He'd heard this and that from his mother, Mrs. Cable. He said Louise almost died. He said it right in front of Louise. It's not the kind of thing you say about people, but Louise didn't seem to mind. That was Louise.

I thought he was going to wonder why Mother couldn't be cleaning up their house. I was thinking, "He's going to know about Mother having that other job." So I thought, "Now we're going to see some trouble."

He was asking about the dippers, because he'd heard about them coming up but they didn't have them around where he lived. He knew there were a lot of them where we were down near the river. I was telling him this and telling him that, but the dippers were mostly gone by then.

He kept saying, "When do you think Marjorie will be back?" He was talking and talking. He said, "What school do you go to?" Then Aunt Benedict came out and she said to him, "Now, you run along home." I thought, "He knows," but he didn't catch on.

Mother used to say to me, "You think every little thing is the end of the world."

When Louise got better she still couldn't use that leg, because it turns out it was the paralysis. That's what happened to her leg.

But Louise never seemed to bother too much about it. Once she could get around, she never seemed to take too much notice. She went on the same as usual.

It's one of those things that looks worse than it really is. And Louise was always one to look on the bright side of things.

By that fall, she could get around pretty good.

Barbara Nichol thanks, for the book's existence, Eleanor Wachtel and Sandra Rabinovitch of CBC Radio's *Writers and Company*, Kathy Lowinger, and Malcolm Lester. For its Ontario spirit she is indebted to her beloved mother, Elizabeth Nichol, and her dear friend, Joseph Martin Arquette.

Published in Canada by Tundra Books, 481 University Avenue,
Toronto, Ontario, M5G 2E9

Published in the United States by Tundra Books of Northern New York,
P.O. Box 1030, Plattsburgh, N.Y., 12901

Library of Congress Catalog Number: 96-61695

Canadian Cataloguing in Publication Data

Nichol, Barbara (Barbara Susan Lang)
Dippers

ISBN 0-88776-396-0

I. Moser, Barry. II. Title.

PS8577.I165D56 1997 jC813´.54 C96-932285-2
PZ7.N52Di 1997

The publisher has applied funds from its Canada Council grant for 1997 toward the editing and production of this book.

Design: Barry Moser

Printed and bound in Canada

01 00 99 98 97 5 4 3 2 1